Autumn
Publishing

Published in 2018
by Autumn Publishing
Cottage Farm
Sywell
NN6 0BJ
www.igloobooks.com

TOP002 0818
2 4 6 8 10 9 7 5 3 1
ISBN 978-1-78810-254-4

Printed and manufactured in China

Disney · PIXAR

STORYBOOK COLLECTION

Autumn
Publishing

Contents

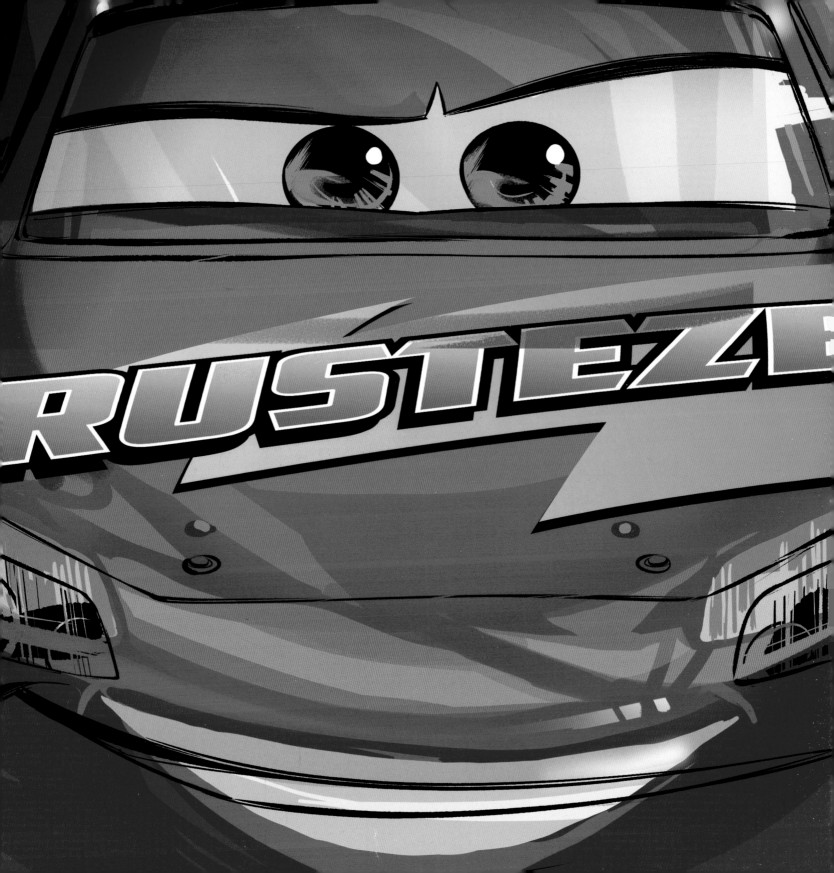

Lightning McQueen's racing season was off to a flying start. The hotshot racer had his sights set on another cup victory.

Lightning's first race of the season had seen him fly across the finish line to take the chequered flag ahead of his rivals, Cal Weathers and Bobby Swift.

The next race in Arizona saw Lightning tear up the track, just as before. This time, with one lap to go, McQueen and Swift were going head-to-head.

But as the flag came out, a slick black racer made his move. Jackson Storm zoomed over the line to take the victory.

"What a pleasure it is to finally beat you!" Storm teased Lightning after the race.

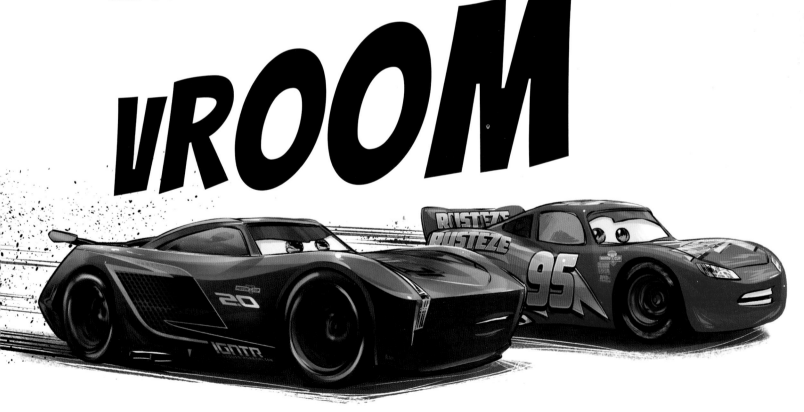

Storm increased his lead as the season continued, beating McQueen every time. No matter how hard he revved his engine, Lightning just couldn't keep up.

The racing world was changing and the next generation of high-tech racers were faster and stronger. His old friend Cal Weathers retired and Brick Yardley was replaced by a Next Gen.

But Lightning wasn't about to give up – he loved racing too much. By the time the last race of the season came round, he had a plan to beat Storm.

If Lightning made a steady start, he could save his speed to overtake Storm in the final laps.

Lightning zoomed out of the pits with new tyres and plenty

of fuel to take the lead. Lightning pushed as hard as he could,

but Storm quickly caught up.

"Enjoy your retirement!" Storm laughed, as he sped past McQueen.

Lightning pushed himself to the max until, suddenly, one of his tyres blew. His friends in the crowd gasped as Lightning lost control and went spinning across the track.

He flipped into the air in a cloud of sparks and smoke. CRAASH! At last, a terrified Lightning skidded to a stop.

CRA

Months passed as Lightning sat alone in Doc's garage in Radiator Springs.

"It's safe to say that Lightning McQueen's racing days are over,"

the radio crackled.

Lightning switched off the radio and watched a film of a race –

the one where Doc Hudson, his old crew chief and mentor, had crashed.

Lightning hadn't raced since his own big crash. But he decided that he

wasn't ready to quit just yet. He had to speak to his

Rust-eze sponsors, Dusty and Rusty.

The next day, Lightning travelled to the brand-new Rust-eze

Racing Centre to discover that Dusty and Rusty had sold Rust-eze

and the number 95 to a business car named Sterling.

Sterling showed Lightning around the racing centre. Lightning

was amazed – he'd never seen anything like it before.

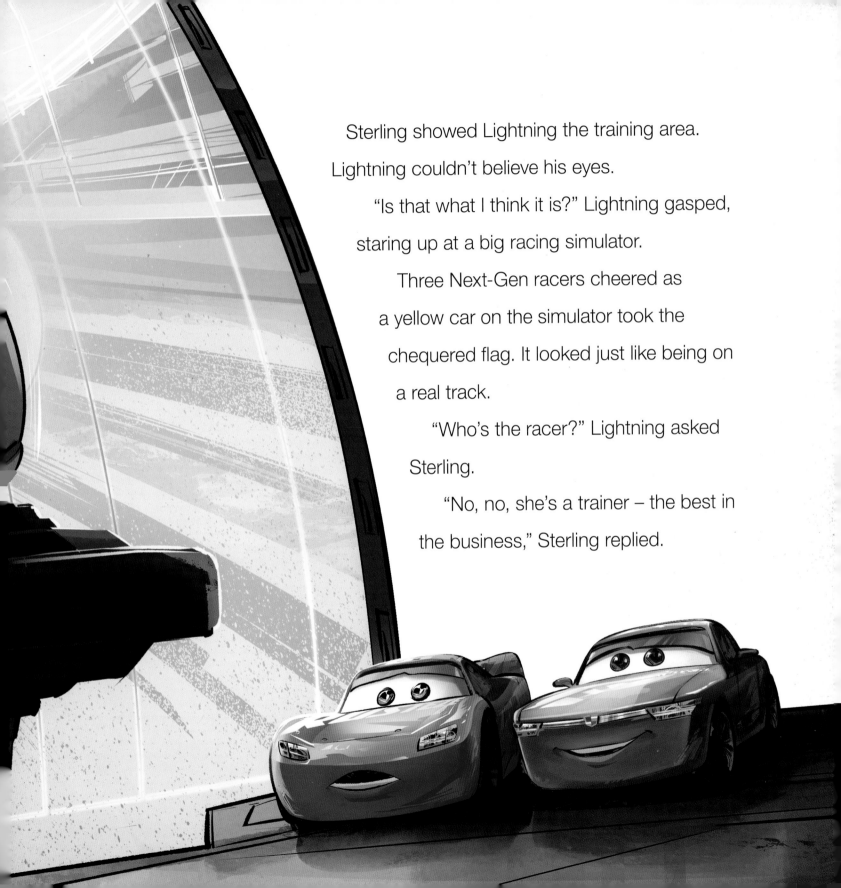

Sterling showed Lightning the training area. Lightning couldn't believe his eyes.

"Is that what I think it is?" Lightning gasped, staring up at a big racing simulator.

Three Next-Gen racers cheered as a yellow car on the simulator took the chequered flag. It looked just like being on a real track.

"Who's the racer?" Lightning asked Sterling.

"No, no, she's a trainer – the best in the business," Sterling replied.

Cruz Ramirez was going to be Lightning's new trainer. She was a cool and calm car. If anyone could help Lightning make a comeback, it was Cruz!

Lightning was bursting to get going on the simulator, but Cruz had other ideas.

"We need to save your energy," Cruz explained. "We'll work on your speed after your nap."

But when Lightning saw his chance, he sped away from Cruz and drove up the simulator ramp.

Sterling arrived to watch his star racer in action. But Lightning lost control and crashed through the simulator screen!

Sterling wanted Lightning to give up racing and get rich making TV adverts and promoting racing merchandise instead. But Lightning begged for another chance to race.

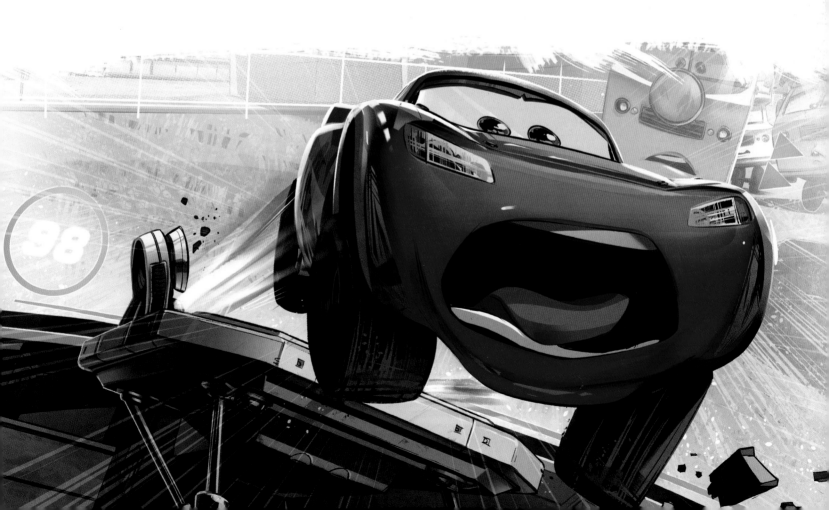

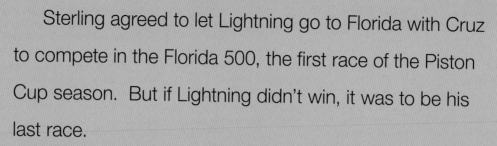

Sterling agreed to let Lightning go to Florida with Cruz to compete in the Florida 500, the first race of the Piston Cup season. But if Lightning didn't win, it was to be his last race.

Lightning was done with treadmills and simulators – he needed to train his own way and get his tyres dirty.

Lightning and Cruz headed out onto Fireball Beach to start training.

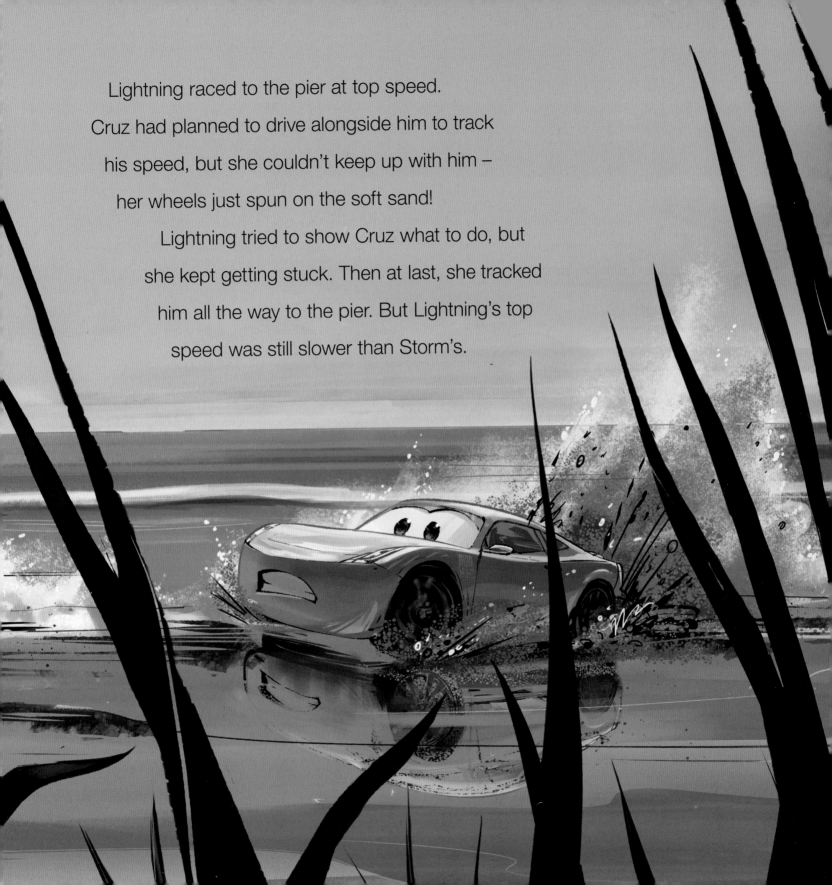

Lightning raced to the pier at top speed.
Cruz had planned to drive alongside him to track
his speed, but she couldn't keep up with him –
her wheels just spun on the soft sand!

Lightning tried to show Cruz what to do, but
she kept getting stuck. Then at last, she tracked
him all the way to the pier. But Lightning's top
speed was still slower than Storm's.

Lightning needed to race against real racers. When he spotted a sign for the Thunder Hollow Speedway, he had an idea. He would race at the track there in disguise – he didn't want the cameras following his every move.

Soon, Mack's trailer was transformed into a party supplies truck and Lightning was covered from bumper to bumper in mud.

Lightning's famous number 95 was now a muddy number 15. Cruz was also disguised as a racer with a 20 sprayed on her side. Together, they rolled up to the speedway just as the race was starting.

Lightning and Cruz met some of the other racers on the track, including a terrifying school bus called Miss Fritter.

Lightning joined the race as 'Chester Whipplefilter'. Meanwhile, Cruz introduced herself as 'Frances Beltline'. She had planned to track Lightning's speed from the middle of the stadium, but she was forced to join the race.

"Welcome to Thunder Hollow for tonight's C-raa-zyy Eight!" the announcer boomed.

Lightning and Cruz looked at each other, scared, as stacks of tyres exploded and cars began to smash into each other all around them. This wasn't a normal race – it was a demolition derby and there was no escape.

"Make way for the undefeated champion – Miss Fritter!" the announcer roared, as the fierce schoolbus thundered onto the track and charged towards Cruz. Cruz couldn't move – she was frozen with fear. But Lightning spotted the danger and pushed Cruz to safety.

The action continued until Cruz swerved past a huge water tanker causing him to tip over. Lightning was sprayed with water and his muddy disguise washed away.

"It's Lightning McQueen!" gasped a fan in the crowd.

After the race, Lightning was not impressed. None of Cruz's training had helped improve his speed.

"This is my last chance, Cruz!" he said, angrily. "If you were a racer, you'd know what I'm talking about. But you're not."

"I wanted to become a racer forever," said Cruz. "But the other racers were bigger and stronger – I didn't belong."

She wished him good luck, before speeding away back to the Rust-eze Racing Centre.

Later, inside Mack's trailer, Lightning couldn't sleep.
He missed home, so he decided to call his friend, Mater.

"Tell me what the problem is and we'll fix it," Mater smiled.

Lightning sighed. He wished Doc Hudson was still around –
Doc could could always fix his problems.

"There was nobody smarter
than old Doc," Mater agreed.
"Except for maybe whoever
taught him."

That was it!
Lightning had to find
Doc's old crew chief
– Smokey.

The next morning, Mack and Lightning headed for Thomasville – Doc Hudson's hometown racetrack. But first, they had to find Cruz. Lightning felt terrible for shouting at his friend. Mack soon spotted her out on the open road.

"Come with us," Lightning said to Cruz. "I'm sorry I yelled."

Cruz came on board and Lightning told her about his plan to find Smokey.

The old Thomasville track was no longer in operation, but it was still perfect for racing. Lightning and Cruz whipped around the track.

But as they skidded round the bend, the cars had to brake hard. A figure stood before them on the track. It was Smokey!

Smokey introduced Lightning and Cruz to his friends: three racing legends who had competed with Doc.

Then, he told a story about a famous race, where Doc had flipped over another racer to take the victory! Lightning and Cruz were amazed.

To beat Storm, Lightning was going to need a racing partner. So, Guido and the Legends fitted a spoiler and racing tyres to Cruz and transformed her into 'Jackson Storm 2.0'! She was ready to go, but this time as a racer, not a trainer.

Smokey gave Cruz a head start. Lightning sped after her but he couldn't catch up. There was work to do if Lightning was going to beat the real Storm.

Smokey trained Lightning and Cruz hard. They pulled heavy trailers, dodged bales of hay and even steered through a stampede of tractors. Lightning was feeling better than ever.

In their last practice before the big race, Lightning went out fast, but Cruz caught up and left him for dust.

Lightning was stunned. Even after all his hard work, he still wasn't fast enough. But it was too late for another race – it was time to head to Florida.

The day of the Florida 500 race arrived. Cruz and all Lightning's friends had come to watch.

Lightning rolled to the back of the grid. To everyone's surprise, Lightning made a speedy start.

"Show 'em how the old guys race!" shouted Smokey, who was acting as Lightning's crew chief. Lightning pushed hard and began overtaking the racers in front.

In the pits, Sterling ordered Cruz to take off her racing tyres and head back to the training centre. "You're a trainer, Cruz. Not a racer," he said.

Lightning heard Sterling's harsh words over his headset. As he raced, all he could think about was Cruz: her speed on the simulator, all their races in training and how Cruz had beaten him every time.

Suddenly, two cars crashed up ahead. Lightning swerved and headed immediately into the pits.

"I need Cruz back here!" he told Smokey. Cruz was a racer, no matter what anyone said.

A puzzled Cruz rolled into the pit lane. Lightning told his team to work on Cruz instead of him.

Guido, Luigi and Ramone worked fast and soon, Cruz was ready. Her spoiler shined and the number 95 glistened on her side. She looked like a racer from bumper to bumper.

"Today's the day, Cruz. You're getting your shot," Lightning told her. "I started this race and you're going to finish it."

As the race resumed, everyone was amazed to see a different number 95 on the track. The green flag dropped and they were off!

Cruz started slowly, but Lightning knew what to do.

Lightning asked Smokey to tell Cruz to remember their Thomasville training and imagine the other cars as tractors.

Cruz looked for spaces to steer around the other racers. The plan worked and Cruz began overtaking the cars one by one!

On the final lap, Cruz drew up alongside Storm.

She tried to pass him, but Storm spotted the move

and rammed her against a wall.

"You don't belong on this track!" he yelled.

"YES... I... DO!" she shouted back.

Remembering Doc's move, Cruz flipped up and over Storm.

She touched down again on the track in front of Storm and then

crossed the finish line in first place!

The crowd went wild,

and Lightning couldn't have been more proud.

Then, it was announced that Cruz and Lightning were joint-winners because

Lightning had started the race. Lightning hadn't lost, so he didn't have to retire!

He knew his racing days weren't over, but for now, Lightning was devoted to

getting Cruz ready for her next big race. It didn't matter who was the racer and

who was the trainer, Lightning and Cruz were both true champions.

Dory was a little blue tang who lived with her parents. From a very young age, Dory had trouble remembering things.

"Hi, I'm Dory," she would say. "I have short-term memory loss."

Dory's mum and dad did everything they could to stop her from getting lost. But one day, Dory couldn't find her way back to them!

Dory kept on swimming, getting further away from her home. She asked every fish she met if they had seen her parents. None of them had.

"Hi, I've lost my family," Dory would say. "Can you help me?"

"Where did you see them last?" the fish would ask.

"Funny story, but... I forgot."

Dory couldn't remember where she came from.

On her journey, Dory met a clownfish called Marlin.

Kind-hearted Dory helped Marlin find his missing son, Nemo.

A year later, long after Nemo was found, the three friends

lived together on the coral reef. Their underwater home was full

of colour and they had lots of fun together.

Then suddenly everything changed. Dory was
swept away in a strong current caused by a group of
migrating stingrays. Her world spun around her and
then faded to black.

While she was knocked out, Dory muttered:
"The Jewel of Morro Bay, California."

She woke up to a flood of memories.
Now, she remembered her parents and her home
– she was from California!

Dory asked Marlin and Nemo to travel across the ocean with her to find her parents. They hitched a ride to California with their old friend, Crush the turtle, and soon arrived in Morro Bay, ready to start their search.

But before they could begin, Dory was scooped up by a human and
carried away in a boat!

A voice came over a loudspeaker: "Welcome to the Marine Life Institute.
We believe in Rescue, Rehabilitation and Release."

At the Institute, Dory had a tag clipped to her fin and was dropped into a water tank.

An octopus reached out a tentacle. "Name's Hank," he said.

Hank explained that Dory was in Quarantine, and the transport tag on her fin meant she was going to be taken to an aquarium in Cleveland.

"Cleveland!" gasped Dory. "No, I can't go to the Cleveland! I have to get to the Jewel of Morro Bay, California…"

Hank said he would help Dory search for her parents if she gave him her transport tag. He liked the idea of living in a nice, safe tank in Cleveland – he didn't want to be sent back to the ocean. Dory agreed to the deal, so Hank scooped her into a coffee pot filled with water and the two of them set off together to find Dory's parents.

As they were deciding where to look, a member of staff appeared.

Hank hid, but Dory read the word on the staff member's bucket.

It said 'DESTINY'. Suddenly, Dory felt she needed to get into that bucket –
so she did! Hank followed as fast as he could as Dory was carried away.

Dory was tipped into a pool with a whale shark called Destiny. Just then, Dory remembered that she had lived in the Open Ocean exhibit next door. She used to talk to Destiny through the pipes when they were young.

The only way to get to the Open Ocean exhibit was by swimming through the pipes, but Dory was afraid she would get lost.

Then Dory remembered her dad used to say there was always another way.

Just then, Dory spotted some pushchairs on the side
of Destiny's pool. "There!" said Dory. "We're gonna hijack
one of those!"

She leapt into a small cup of water on the tray of one
of the pushchairs and Hank pushed her across the
park to the Open Ocean exhibit.

"Now go and get your family," Hank said.

With that, Dory gave Hank her orange tag
and he gently dropped her in the water.

Dory swam towards a trail of shells she remembered seeing when she was a child.

She gasped – this was her home! Her parents had made the shell path to guide her back whenever she got lost.

There was an entrance to a pipe and she remembered her parents warning her not to go near it, as the strong current would carry her away. Young Dory had forgotten and been sucked into the pipe!

"It was my fault," Dory whispered. "My parents… I lost them."

Dory swam in circles, not sure what to do next!

A friendly crab explained that all the blue tangs had been taken to Quarantine, ready to be shipped to the aquarium in Cleveland. Dory couldn't believe it!

The only way back to Quarantine was through the pipes, so Dory nervously swam in... and was soon lost.

Two shapes emerged from the darkness. Marlin and Nemo! A bird called Becky had carried them in a bucket to the Marine Life Institute to search for Dory.

When Marlin, Nemo and Dory finally reached Quarantine, the tank of blue tangs was about to be loaded on the van to Cleveland!

Luckily, Hank was there to help. He quickly dropped Dory and her friends into the tank.

The other blue tangs told Dory that her parents had gone to Quarantine years ago. Nobody knew what had happened to them.

Dory was heartbroken. Hank scooped her back up in a coffee pot.

But Marlin and Nemo were still inside
the tank. Someone grabbed Hank and bundled him
into the van. The coffee pot shattered and Dory slid
into a drain, which took her back into the ocean.
Once again, Dory was alone.

Dory swam out in the bay, then something caught her eye – a shell trail.

Suddenly, two blue tangs appeared. Dory gasped. Her parents!

Dory's parents had been creating shell pathways all this time, in the hope that

Dory would see them and remember.

"It's you! It's really you!" cried Dory as she burst into tears.

"Oh, honey, you found us," said Dory's mum. "And you know why you found us? Because you remembered. You remembered in your own amazing Dory way."

Dory was so happy, but she hadn't forgotten her other family, Marlin and Nemo. She had to save them!

With help from Destiny, Dory caught up with the van that was carrying Marlin, Nemo and Hank. Destiny used her tail to flip Dory up to the van and Hank helped Dory into the tank.

"Dory! You came back!" Nemo cried.

Dory smiled. "Of course. I couldn't leave my family."

Marlin called for Becky the bird. She scooped up Marlin and Nemo, but left Dory behind!

The van sped off with Dory and Hank trapped inside! Hank quickly slid through a vent in the roof and down onto the windscreen.

The shocked driver pulled over and leapt out. Dory's family watched in amazement as Hank slid into the driver's seat and drove the van off a bridge – and into the ocean!

The doors flew open and the fish spilt out. They were free!

Dory returned to life on the reef. Her blue tang family and all her friends joined her – even Hank. She was happier than she had ever been!

But Marlin was nervous that Dory would get lost again and often followed her. One day, the two of them bobbed in the water at the edge of the reef, gazing out into the blue.

"Wow! It really is quite a view," said Marlin.

Dory looked back towards her home and saw an even better sight – her whole family, together again.

"Unforgettable," she said.

INSIDE OUT

When a little girl called Riley was born, an Emotion named Joy took control inside Riley's mind. Joy was in charge of a console in Headquarters and she kept Riley happy.

A golden sphere rolled into Headquarters and Joy picked it up. This was Riley's first memory and it showed her as a baby. It was golden because it was a happy memory.

As Riley grew older, Joy was joined by four more Emotions: Fear, Disgust, Anger and Sadness. The Emotions all worked together to help Riley.

When an important event happened, a core memory was created and they powered Riley's Islands of Personality.

There were five islands: Goofball, Friendship, Hockey, Honesty and Family.

When Riley was 11, her mum and dad announced they were moving from their hometown in Minnesota to San Francisco. The Emotions panicked. How would Riley feel about leaving her home and all her friends?

After a long car journey, Riley and her parents arrived at their new house in San Francisco.

Joy tried to keep Riley happy by taking charge of the console that controlled her thoughts.

Soon, it was Riley's first day at her new school.

Joy gave each Emotion an important job to do.

Joy was determined to keep Riley happy on her first day. She drew a circle of chalk on the floor around Sadness.

"This is the circle of sadness – your job today is to make sure that any unhappiness stays inside," she told Sadness.

At school, Riley had to stand up and tell the class about herself.

She began to share a happy memory about playing hockey in Minnesota.

But suddenly, her smile faded.

"You've left the circle!" Joy said to Sadness. "You've touched the hockey memory sphere and turned it blue!"

Riley started to cry, creating the first-ever blue core memory.

Joy was furious! She pressed a button and a tube began to suck away the blue sphere. But in the chaos, all six core memories were sucked up the tube – as well as Joy and Sadness!

The two Emotions were dumped faraway in Riley's mind. The Islands of Personality had turned dark, since the core memories weren't in the holder to power them up. Joy knew they had to get the memories back to Headquarters so the Islands would work again.

But Headquarters was far away. Joy collected the five yellow core memories. She and Sadness headed across a bridge to Goofball Island.

"But what if we fall down into the Memory Dump?" asked Sadness. "We'd be forgotten about forever!"

"We won't fall," Joy replied. "Just think positive."

In Headquarters, Anger took control of the console. Riley became cross with her dad and she refused to goof around with him. Suddenly, Goofball Island began to collapse!

Joy quickly grabbed Sadness and they made it to safety before the island disappeared into the Memory Dump.

Joy tried to stay positive – they could make their way to another island through the winding shelves of Long Term Memory, where millions of memories were stored. But Sadness slumped to the floor in despair. She realised that they could lose the other Islands of Personality. Joy picked up one of her legs and dragged her along.

Anger was still driving the console as Riley chatted to her old friend Meg on her laptop. Meg told her about a new girl on the hockey team. Riley missed playing hockey with her old friends, so this news made her angry. Flames roared out of the top of Anger's head and Riley slammed her laptop shut.

Back in Long Term Memory, Joy and Sadness heard a loud groan as Friendship Island fell into the dump.

"Goodbye friendship, hello loneliness," said Sadness.

Joy looked up to Hockey Island. "We'll just have to go the long way round," she said, trying hard to stay cheery.

77

On their way to Hockey Island, Joy and Sadness bumped into a funny-looking creature with legs like a cat and a trunk like an elephant.

"You're Bing Bong!" Joy said. "You were Riley's imaginary friend."

Riley and Bing Bong used to play together – they had a rocket wagon that was powered by a song. But over the years, Riley had forgotten him.

Bing Bong was in Long Term Memory looking for a good memory, so Riley would remember him and he could be part of her life again.

"We're on our way to Headquarters. Come with us and we'll get Riley to remember you," said Joy.

Bing Bong gave his bag to Joy to help her carry the core memories. He told Joy and Sadness that it would be quicker to catch the Train of Thought from Imagination Land to Headquarters.

The three of them arrived at the platform just as the train pulled away, but Bing Bong knew how to get to another station.

When they walked inside Imagination Land, Joy and Sadness were amazed! There was a Trophy Town, a French Fry Forest and a Cloud Town.

They reached a House of Cards, where Bing Bong found his rocket wagon.

Meanwhile, Riley was at the try-outs for a new hockey team.

At Headquarters, Anger, Disgust and Fear tried to get Riley through it. But the Emotions couldn't find the right memory to help Riley play hockey. Riley missed the puck, fell over and stormed off the rink.

Inside Riley's mind, Hockey Island sank into the Memory Dump. Joy, Sadness and Bing Bong watched in horror from the gates of Preschool World.

Inside Preschool World, some Mind Workers took Bing Bong's rocket wagon and threw it into the Memory Dump.

"No!" yelled Bing Bong. He sat on the floor and cried sweets. Joy tried to cheer him up, but nothing worked.

Sadness sat beside him. "I'm sorry they took your rocket wagon," she said.

After they talked about how he felt, he said, "I'm okay now."

Joy was surprised – Sadness had made Bing Bong feel better.

Joy, Sadness and Bing Bong finally made it to the train, but it soon stopped because Riley had gone to sleep.

To wake her up and get the train moving again, Joy and Sadness found a huge, scary clown called Jangles hidden in Riley's Subconscious – where her darkest fears lived. They led Jangles to Dream Productions, where Riley's dreams were made. The clown crashed into Riley's head and she woke up with a start!

The three of them ran back to the train and jumped aboard as it started moving again.

Meanwhile, at Headquarters, Anger decided that Riley should run away – back to Minnesota. As he plugged an idea bulb into the console, the idea popped into Riley's head.

Riley needed to buy a bus ticket to Minnesota, so she sneaked downstairs and took money from her mum's purse.

Back on the Train of Thought, Joy heard a noise. She looked out
of the train carriage to see Honesty Island fall into the dump.

Suddenly, the tracks crumbled away and the train crashed. Everyone leapt
free of the train, as it tipped over the cliff into the Memory Dump.

"That was our way home!" Joy cried. "We've just lost another island.
What's happening?"

"Haven't you heard?" replied a train worker. "Riley is running away."

After the train crash, Sadness realised they could use a recall tube in Long Term Memory to get back to Headquarters. But, as Joy got sucked up the tube, the cliff underneath them began to break apart. The tube broke and Joy fell deep into the Memory Dump!

At that moment, Riley was heading to the bus station, feeling nothing.

Down in the dump, Joy looked at a memory of a time when Riley had been sad, but her friends had cheered her up. Joy realised that Sadness was important – Riley's friends came to help because she was sad!

Just then, Bing Bong appeared. The pair came up with an idea – they could use Bing Bong's rocket wagon to fly out of the Memory Dump!

They sang loudly to power the rocket, but each time they flew up, they couldn't reach the top of the cliff.

The friends gave it one last try and, without Joy noticing, Bing Bong jumped out of the rocket wagon so it could make it to the top.

As Joy looked back, she saw Bing Bong in the dump far below.

"Go save Riley!" he called. "Take her to the moon for me, okay?"

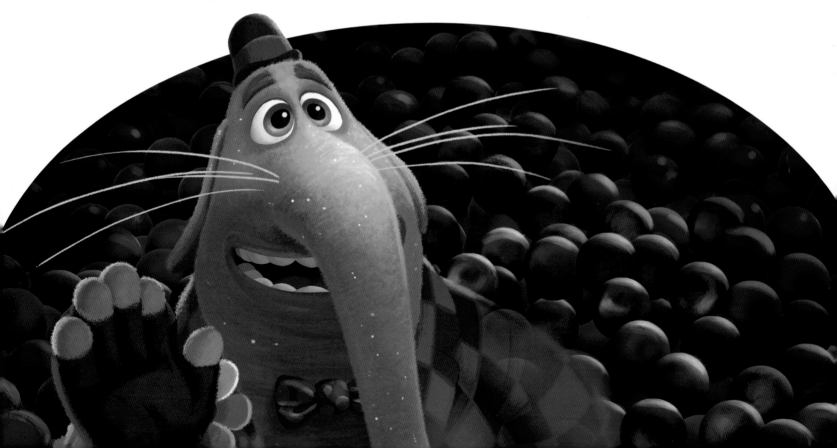

Joy spotted Sadness floating away on a cloud.

"I only make everything worse," said Sadness.

Joy had to reach her.

Using the Imaginary Boyfriend Generator from
Imagination Land, she made a tall tower
of boyfriends. Joy climbed up it and swung
towards Sadness…

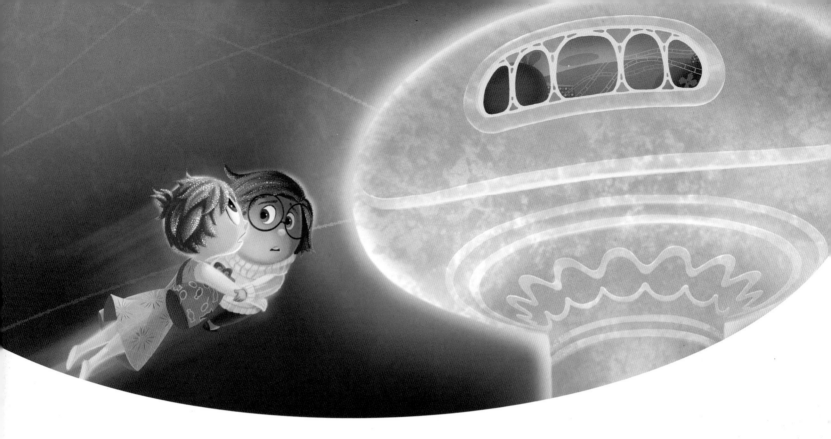

Joy grabbed hold of Sadness and they flew through the air together towards Headquarters. SPLAT! They hit the back window and started to slide down the glass.

Anger, Fear and Disgust ran towards the window. How were they going to get their friends inside?

Disgust had an idea! She got Anger really mad until flames burst out of his head. She used the fire to cut a hole in the window. Joy and Sadness climbed inside.

"Oh, thank goodness you're back!" cried Fear.

Joy looked up at the screen and saw that Riley was on the bus, ready to run away back to Minnesota. Joy realised that she had to let Sadness take control. Sadness stepped up to the console. She pulled out the idea bulb. On the bus, Riley suddenly felt very sad. She wanted to go home.

"Wait!" she called to the driver. "I want to get off!"

As the other Emotions looked on, Joy handed the core memories to Sadness and they all turned blue. Sadness placed them in the projector that played memories on the screen in Headquarters.

Riley arrived back home and told her mum and dad how she felt.

"I miss home," she said, remembering her life back in Minnesota. She began to cry.

Riley, Mum and Dad hugged each other and, at Headquarters, a new core memory was created, which built a brand-new Family Island.

A few days later, the Islands of Personality had reappeared – with a few new ones, too! Joy, Sadness, Anger, Fear and Disgust were excited about the future. After all, Riley was 12 now... anything could happen next.

A long time ago, there lived two dinosaurs called Henry and Ida. They lived on a farm with their three children – Buck, Libby and Arlo.

Arlo was the youngest and he was afraid of everything. Most of all, Arlo was afraid of the wilderness beyond the family's farm.

One night, Henry took Arlo into the field. Suddenly, an insect landed on Arlo's nose. He was scared, but Poppa blew gently on the insect – and it glowed!

Then, Poppa swept his tail through the grass and hundreds of fireflies flew into the sky. Arlo was amazed.

One day, Poppa discovered a little critter eating their food.

"You're gonna catch that critter," he told Arlo.

Arlo was afraid, but wanted to make his dad proud. He heard the

critter in Poppa's trap – it was a human boy! Arlo set him free.

When Poppa saw the empty trap, he took Arlo to find the critter.

But a storm set in and Poppa was swept away in a flood!

With Poppa gone, the family had to work hard on the farm.

Arlo was determined to help take care of his family.

It wasn't long before Arlo caught the critter stealing corn again.
As he and the critter fought, they tumbled backwards into the river.

"Mum!" Arlo cried, but he had been swept too far away for anyone to
hear. The river carried Arlo away. Then – BAM! The little dinosaur hit his
head on a rock and he was pulled under by the current.

When Arlo woke up, he had no idea where he was.

He was alone and the wilderness was all around him.

Suddenly, Arlo heard a howl. Standing on the

clifftop above him was the critter.

"You!" shouted Arlo. "This is all your fault!"

Furious, he tried to climb up the cliff to get at the critter. But the critter wasn't afraid.

The critter ran off, leaving the dinosaur all alone. Arlo was scared.

Before long, it started to get dark and heavy raindrops fell from the sky.

Arlo built a shelter using branches and he curled up beneath its leaky roof.

Then, he heard a rustling in the bushes. It was heading towards him.

It was… the critter! He had brought Arlo a branch of berries. The two of them became friends.

Arlo gave the boy a name – Spot. Even though Spot couldn't talk, he and Arlo found a way of communicating. Arlo learned that Spot had lost his family, just as the dinosaur had lost his Poppa.

A few days later, Arlo and Spot met a family of T. rexes called Butch, Ramsey and Nash. They had lost their herd of longhorns.

Arlo offered to help the T. rexes if they could show him the way home. Butch agreed and Spot tracked down the longhorns. But a nasty surprise was waiting for them…

Raptors! These feathery crooks had stolen the longhorns and weren't going to give them up without a fight. Brave Arlo helped stop the raptors.

"You're one tough kid," Butch told Arlo.

As promised, the T. rexes helped Arlo and Spot find the way home and the pair continued on their journey.

Spot climbed on top of Arlo's head and pointed towards the sky. Above the clouds was the most beautiful sunset they had ever seen.

As Arlo and Spot made
their way along the mountain pass, a storm was brewing.

Suddenly, a pack of Pterodactyls swooped down.

They caught hold of Spot and whisked him out of sight!

Arlo chased after the Pterodactyls and drove them away. But Spot

was now trapped down river and the water was rising.

The storm was raging now,

and suddenly the river burst its banks!

Arlo and Spot were swept away in

the flood. The dinosaur could see his friend, but he couldn't reach

him. Arlo grabbed Spot just as they tumbled over a waterfall. The two

friends clung to each other as they fell into the river far below.

Arlo climbed on to the shore holding his friend. They were safe.

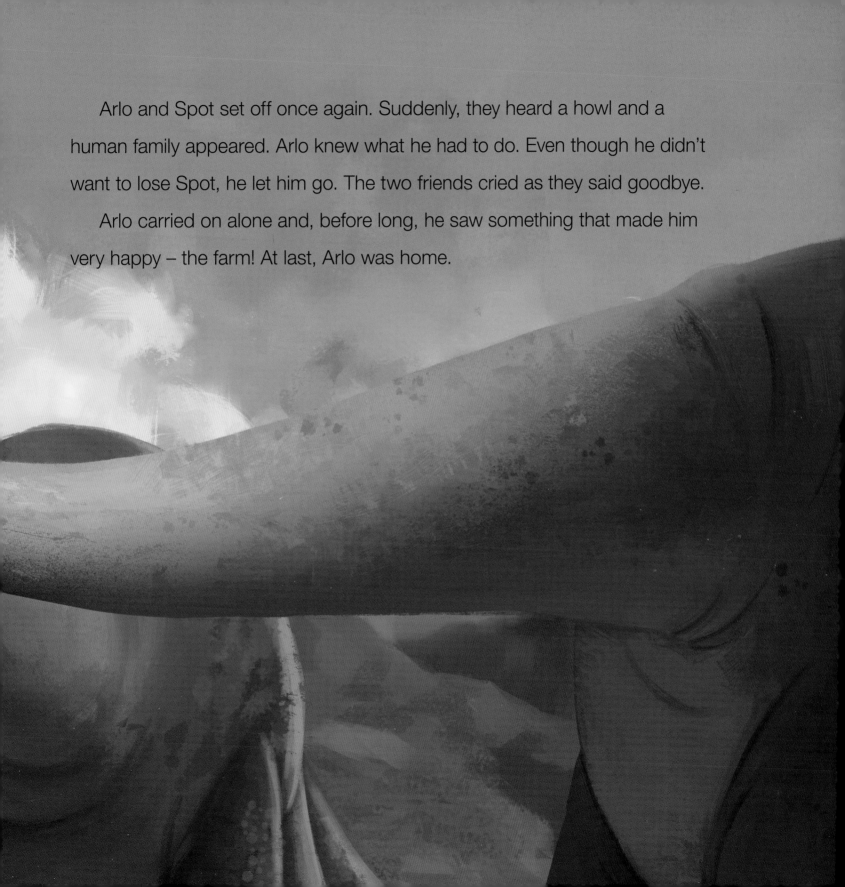

Arlo and Spot set off once again. Suddenly, they heard a howl and a human family appeared. Arlo knew what he had to do. Even though he didn't want to lose Spot, he let him go. The two friends cried as they said goodbye. Arlo carried on alone and, before long, he saw something that made him very happy – the farm! At last, Arlo was home.

Andy loved his toys and they loved him. Sheriff Woody, Buzz Lightyear, Jessie the cowgirl, Rex and Hamm were happiest when they were on one of Andy's adventures. For the toys, playing with Andy was the best feeling in the world.

But as Andy grew, he played with the toys less and less. By the time he was getting ready for college, the toys were worried. Woody tried to reassure everyone. Andy would tuck them all in the attic for safekeeping, he explained.

Andy's mum had another idea. She suggested that Andy donate his old toys to a daycare centre.

"No one's going to want those," he told her. "They're junk."

Andy dumped Rex, Hamm, Slinky and Mr and Mrs Potato Head into a rubbish bag! He glanced at his two favourites, Buzz and Woody. He dropped Woody into a box marked 'College' – and Buzz went into the rubbish bag.

The toys thought they were heading for the bin, but Andy planned to put the bag in the attic. Then, Andy's mum made a mistake. She thought the bag was rubbish and left it at the kerb.

Frantic, Woody climbed out of the window to help his friends. He watched as the binman hurled the bags into the back of the bin lorry and crushed the entire load with the rubbish compactor!

Then Woody noticed an upside-down recycling bin moving across Andy's driveway. His friends had escaped!

Inside the garage, the toys were upset and confused. Andy had thrown them away.

Jessie had an idea. They should go to the daycare centre. Everyone climbed inside the box of old toys that Andy's mum was taking to daycare.

Woody followed his friends into the box. He tried to explain about the rubbish bag mix-up, but the toys didn't believe him.

SLAM! Andy's mum shut the car boot and started driving.

Soon, the toys arrived at Sunnyside Daycare. Andy's toys were taken to the Butterfly Room where they were welcomed by the daycare toys.

There was a big, pink bear who smelt like strawberries. "Welcome to Sunnyside!" he cried. "I'm Lots-o'-Huggin' Bear! But, please, call me Lotso!"

"Mr Lotso," said Rex. "Do toys here get played with every day?"

"All day long," Lotso answered. "When the kids get old, new ones come in. No owners means no heartbreak."

Lotso and a doll named Big Baby gave the toys a tour before taking them to their new home at Sunnyside – the Caterpillar Room.

Woody begged his friends not to stay. They belonged at Andy's house.

But the others disagreed. "We have a new life here, Woody," Jessie said.

Woody could see his friends' minds were made up. Feeling sad and unsure, he said goodbye.

He clambered onto the roof and used an old kite to fly over the walls. When he crash-landed, he was bruised, hatless and hanging from a branch.

The receptionist's daughter, Bonnie, ran over to the dangling cowboy and shoved him into her rucksack. Then, she took him home.

Inside the Caterpillar Room, a crowd of toddlers burst in. They tangled Slinky's coil, dipped Jessie's hair in paint and covered Hamm with glitter.

One of the toddlers threw Buzz onto a windowsill. From there, he could see into the Butterfly Room, where older kids were playing gently with Lotso and the other daycare toys. He couldn't understand why Andy's toys been put in the Caterpillar Room. The toddlers' play was too rough.

Finally, the children went home.

"I'll talk to Lotso about moving us to the other room," said Buzz. The toys discovered they were locked in, so Buzz escaped through an open window above the door.

Mrs Potato Head started to see strange images coming to her through the eye she'd lost back at Andy's house.

"Andy's looking in the attic," she said. "Why is he so upset?"

She gasped. "He meant to put us in the attic!" They had to get home!

Buzz found some of the Sunnyside toys inside a vending machine.

He overheard them saying how dangerous the Caterpillar Room was.

Lotso arrived and seemed as friendly as ever. He granted Buzz's request to move to the Butterfly Room – but Buzz's friends had to stay behind.

"I can't accept," said Buzz. "We're family. We stay together."

Suddenly, Lotso changed. He called for the Buzz Lightyear Instruction Manual.

Then, he ordered his gang to reset Buzz's switch to 'Demo Mode'.

When Lotso arrived in the Caterpillar Room, Andy's toys begged to leave.

"Here's the thing," the bear said. "You ain't leaving Sunnyside." Somebody had to put up with the little kids' rough play!

Buzz appeared and accused his old friends of being minions of Zurg!

Jessie and the others were shocked. What had happened to him?

Andy's toys were herded into the room's wire baskets. When Mr Potato Head fought back, Big Baby put him in a sandbox in the playground.

Lotso left Andy's toys under Buzz's guard. The daycare was a prison!

Meanwhile, at Bonnie's house, Woody learnt the truth about Sunnyside Daycare from Chuckles the clown, a toy Bonnie had rescued. Chuckles explained that he, Lotso and Big Baby belonged to a girl named Daisy. One day, the toys were left behind on a trip. Lotso led them home, but Daisy had a new pink bear.

In anger, Lotso tore off the pendant that Daisy had given Big Baby. They went to Sunnyside – where Lotso became a tyrant.

Woody desperately wanted to find a way home to Andy. But after hearing the story about Lotso and Sunnyside, he knew what he had to do…

Woody couldn't leave his friends in Lotso's clutches. He hitched a ride back to Sunnyside in Bonnie's rucksack.

The cowboy found his pals and that night, Woody and Slinky stole the daycare keys. Mr Potato Head distracted Big Baby while the others captured Buzz. The toys tried to reset Buzz's switch – but now Buzz only spoke Spanish!

Despite the hold-ups, everyone made it safely outside to the playground.

The toys all climbed
into the rubbish chute
and slid down,
one by one.

At the end of the
chute, Slinky formed a
bridge across the bin
so his friends could
escape to freedom.

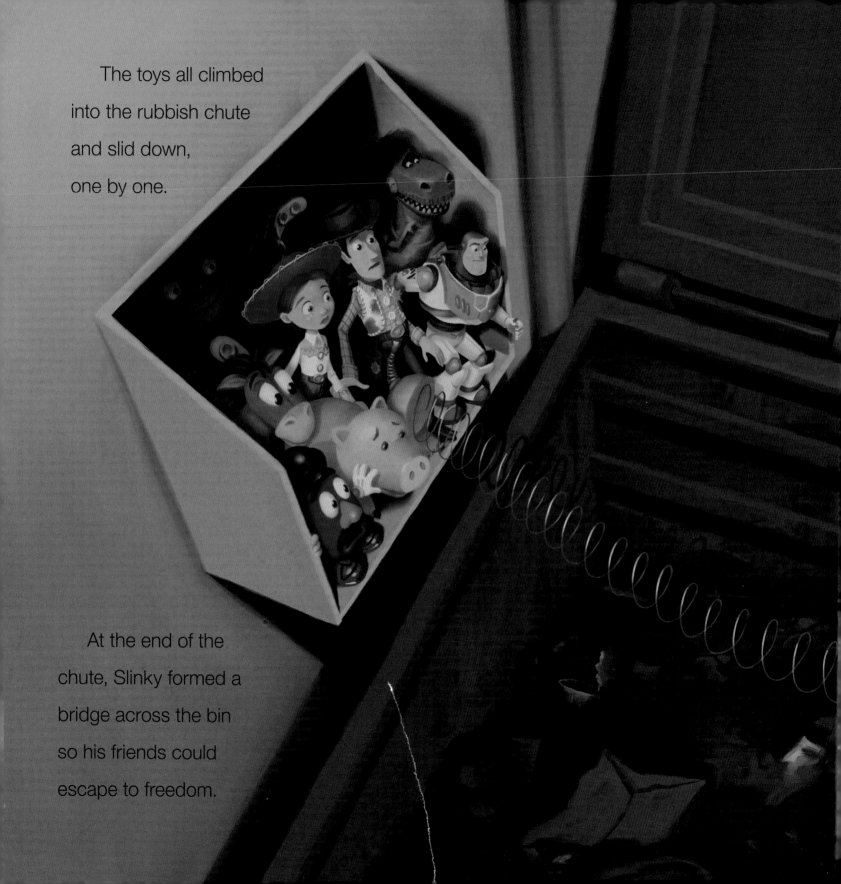

But suddenly, Lotso appeared. "Why don't you come back and join our family again?" he asked the toys.

"You're a liar and a bully and I'd rather rot in this bin than join any family of yours!" Jessie replied.

Lotso scowled. "I didn't throw you away," he replied. "Your kid did. There isn't one kid who ever loved a toy, really."

"What about Daisy?" Woody asked. "She lost you. By accident. She
loved you!" He threw down the old pendant that Chuckles had given him.

"She never loved me!" Lotso exploded. "She left me!"

Big Baby's eyes filled with tears as he thought about Daisy.

"You want your Mummy back? But she never loved you!" Lotso shouted.

Big Baby had heard enough. He hurled Lotso into the rubbish bin!

The daycare toys cheered. Things would be different at Sunnyside now.

"Come on! Hurry!" said Woody, starting to cross the bin lid. He could hear a
rubbish lorry rumbling towards them!

The toys managed to climb up onto a wall to safety. Then, Woody saw an Alien was trapped. The cowboy ran back, but Lotso pulled Woody inside the bin and the lid slammed shut. Andy's toys jumped onto the lid and tried to pull it open, but the rubbish lorry lifted the container and all the toys fell into the lorry!

It rumbled forwards, then lurched to a stop. Rubbish tumbled down on them and a TV landed on top of Buzz. Incredibly, the blow turned him back into his old self!

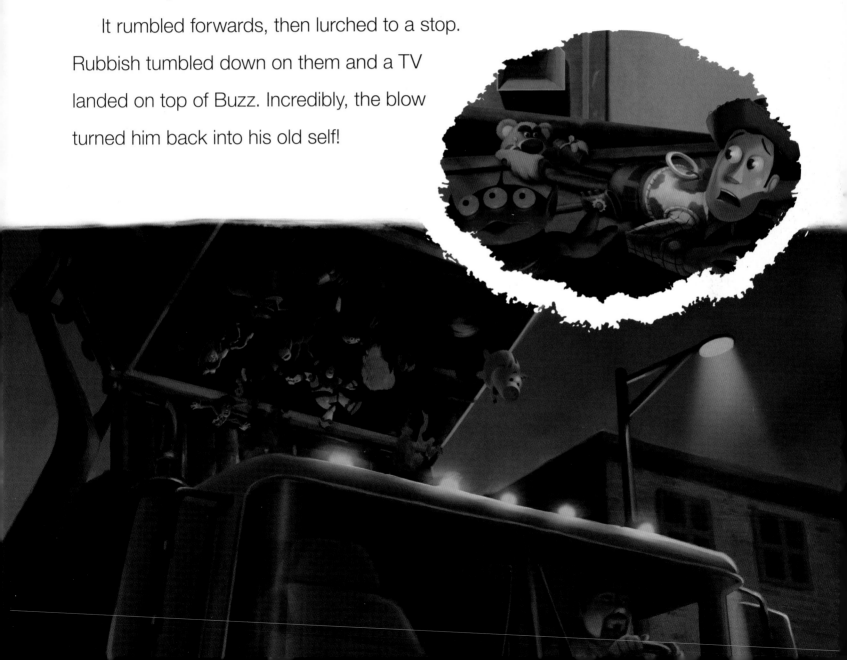

Soon, the lorry arrived at the Tri-County Landfill and dumped its load.

"The claaaaw!" cried the Aliens, as they toddled towards a crane.

Woody went after them, but was cut off. A huge bulldozer pushed the toys into an open pit where they fell onto a conveyor belt. It led to a shredder! But another conveyor belt above them was magnetic. They grabbed onto metal rubbish and were lifted to safety.

But Lotso was trapped! Woody and Buzz dropped back down to free him. The shredder was getting closer and closer...

Woody grabbed Lotso's paw and quickly picked up a metal golf club. Woody, Lotso and Buzz went zooming up to the ceiling. They were safe! But when they joined their friends on another conveyor belt, they soon realised they were now heading towards a burning incinerator!

Lotso managed to find the emergency stop button, but instead of pushing it, he hesitated. Then, a smirk spread across his face and he ran off.

The friends tumbled towards the fire, determined to face it together.

Suddenly, a large shadow passed over the toys. A crane lowered its jaws and scooped them up and away from the fire. Woody looked up to the crane's cab and saw the Aliens inside. They steered the toys over the landfill and dropped them safely to the ground. The Aliens had saved their friends.

Now, the toys had to get Woody home before Andy left for college. Luckily, they spotted their neighbourhood rubbish lorry and jumped on board.

At home, Andy was loading the car. The gang had made it back just in time!

Woody headed for a box marked 'College', while the others climbed into a box marked 'Attic'. Before they separated, Woody and Buzz shook hands.

"You know where to find us, Cowboy," Buzz said finally.

Inside the 'College' box, Woody looked at a photo of Andy with his toys. The cowboy knew that – no matter where they went – they would have the memories of their time together.

Suddenly, he had an idea. He jumped out of the box and wrote a note, which he placed on the attic box.

When Andy grabbed the last boxes, he read the note. He opened the attic box and got a surprise – his toys hadn't been thrown away after all!

A little while later, Andy pulled up at Bonnie's house.

"Someone told me you're really good with toys," Andy said to the little girl.

As Andy introduced his toys to Bonnie, he was startled to find Woody in the box. He wasn't supposed to be there!

"My cowboy!" Bonnie cried.

Andy let Woody stay with Bonnie. From the hug she gave the cowboy, he could see that she loved him.

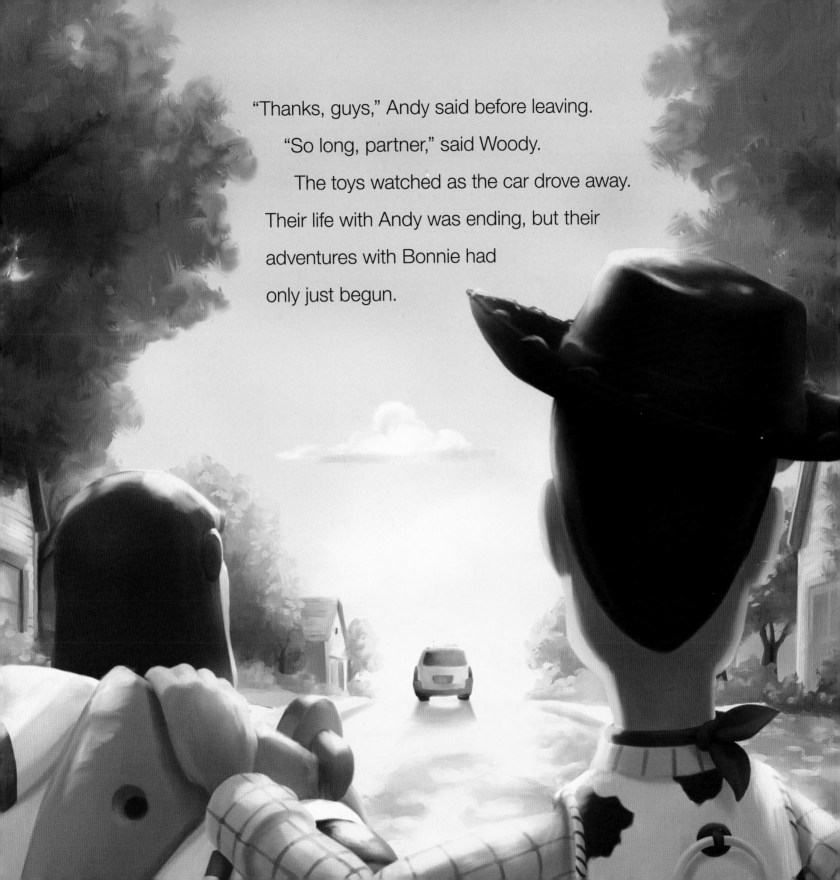

"Thanks, guys," Andy said before leaving.

"So long, partner," said Woody.

The toys watched as the car drove away.

Their life with Andy was ending, but their

adventures with Bonnie had

only just begun.